DELAYED
SATISFACTION

LAUREN BLAKELY

DELAYED SATISFACTION

A PREQUEL NOVELLA TO SATISFACTION GUARANTEED

I'm not looking for love. I'm definitely not even interested in dating. But when I first see the handsome stranger singing on stage and our eyes lock, it feels like kismet. For seven blissful days, we fall into an intoxicating romance. Until one night when I learn just how forbidden we are...

1

_____

Sloane

Networking is such a sexy word.

Not.

But that's my goal for tonight. I arch a brow and consider my outfit in the mirror in my tiny apartment. It's a simple black dress. The neckline isn't too low, so I'd say this number qualifies as classy and sophisticated. It'll do the job, which is—fingers crossed—to help me get a job.

"You look marvelous," my roomie,

Piper, declares, looking up from one of her collections of folders.

"Why, thank you. You look super hot too, poring over all your binders."

She winks. "I won't become the best event planner in the city if I don't know everything about it inside out and upside down."

Her binders contain photos of all the establishments in New York where anyone would ever want to get married or hold a party. Piper points at me. "And you won't be a publicity superstar if you don't get your cute butt in gear."

I waggle my butt. "Damn, that is one fine rear," I say, admiring my tush in the mirror.

Piper pumps a fist. "Body confidence. Own it."

"Amen." We smack palms.

"Also, take these." Piper stands, scurries over to her purse that she left on the couch, and roots around in the Michael Kors knockoff. She tosses a sleeve of condoms at me.

I catch them and shoot her a *you can't be serious* look. "I'm not going to need these tonight. This isn't a pickup event. I'm going to network for job prospects."

She shrugs. "You *might* go to the bone zone."

I roll my eyes. "I won't go to the bone zone."

"Don't be such a pessimist. I have faith in you. I'm betting on you going there. It's been six months, hasn't it?"

"Are you tracking my sex life in your planner? You're such a pervert."

Piper taps her temple. "It's all up here. I track how mean you are to me each month, and it increases exponentially the longer it's been since you've been laid."

I lunge for her like I'm going to put her in a headlock. She darts away. "I am not mean. I am also not horny. I also don't want to"—I stop and sketch air quotes—"*go to bone town*. Or the bone zone. Also, why have you started saying things like *bone zone*?

We live in Hoboken, not a fraternity. Is this because of Axe? Or Jace? Or Dax?"

She wiggles her brows. "It's Jax. And yes. He's such a dude. Everything that comes out of his mouth is *bro* and *babe*. It's great."

I arch a brow. "Why is that great? I thought you loved precise language."

"I do. I love it the same way I love lists and the Oxford comma." Piper returns to her binders and flips a page. "But see, I don't have to worry that Mr. Rugby will ever want anything more. Jax is married to the game, and he has amazing stamina."

"Then, yo yo yo, I'm happy for you getting your brains banged out," I say like a dude.

She chuckles as I dart into the bedroom to grab a pair of chandelier earrings. They're sparkly, and I'm temporarily mesmerized by the prism of light they catch. "But some of us are not as sex-obsessed as you." I return to the living room. "Sure, it's been a while. But I'm not climbing trees or humping walls."

Plus, when my last serious beau, Eddie, ended things unceremoniously because he suddenly decided to move to Los Angeles to hunt for work in the entertainment business, I was shocked. We'd had plans. We were an item.

I'm over him now, thank you very much. I certainly don't miss him anymore, or long for what might have been. But that doesn't mean I'm looking to get back in the saddle. What I want—not tonight and not tomorrow, but someday—is romance. The real deal. Love.

I'm not on the hunt for it now, but I don't need the bone zone either.

I'll know when I've found the genuine article. When I meet a man so romantic I melt from his words, from his touch, from the way he listens and cares. That's what gets me going, rather than the prospect of *amazing stamina*.

But honestly, I'd bet that's what gets Piper going too. She's so focused on work right now that she protects herself by dating guys who have zero interest in anything lasting.

Gathering my clutch purse and tucking a pink lipstick into it, I blow her a kiss. "Will you be here when I get home later?"

She looks up at the ceiling, pretending to think. "Hmm. Will I be here all by my lonesome, or will I be riding a—"

"Okay, then!" I blurt over the details. "Go sow your wild oats, crazy girl."

"You asked."

"I did indeed."

I head to the Luxe Hotel on Fifth Avenue, eager to make some work connections.

Once inside the swank ballroom, that's exactly what I do: mingle with the crowd, chat up several executives at animal rescues, make small talk, and let them know I'm a recent graduate eager to work my way up and willing to prove myself. By the end of two hours, I have quite a stash of business cards in my purse.

My parents are both go-getters. They're outgoing, confident types, and raised me, albeit separately, to be the same way, so I truly don't mind this kind of networking. But after two solid hours of self-selling, I'm ready for a break, so I head to the bar to grab a drink.

Along the way, I survey the scene in the ballroom, taking in the classy guys and gals in suits and tuxes, in lovely frocks and gorgeous shift dresses, chatting and nibbling on hors d'oeuvres. Some are settling in to play table games like poker and blackjack. A karaoke contest has begun. News flash: someone already sang "Livin' On A Prayer."

As I tap my unpolished nails on the counter, considering the bar offerings, a voice floats over the chatter to capture me with a stunning pure tenor that croons, "Isn't it romantic?"

Chills.

I have chills. His voice is straight from a black-and-white movie. He sings like an old-time crooner, and when I turn around, my breath catches, and yes, I nearly melt.

2

Sloane

When I was getting ready, I thought these earrings were mesmerizing.

Mesmerizing?

Puh-leaze.

They're a Kit Kat next to a French artisanal morsel of chocolate.

As I listen to this man sing, I understand the word *mesmerize* in a whole new way, as if his voice is rewriting the dictionary definition at this very moment.

This is the Museum of Modern Art

and gazing upon *Starry Night*. This is opening night at a Broadway show when the lead brings down the house.

This man has that kind of voice.

I feel like Hugh Grant's character in *Love Actually* when he goes searching for Natalie and is asked to sing carols at the houses and his bodyguard or driver—which was he? —turns out to be operatic.

The whole audience here tonight knows they're witnessing a *Love Actually* moment. They're enrapt, stopping their conversations to focus on *that voice*.

The bartender hands me my champagne, and I thank him absently, never taking my eyes off the man onstage, singing kara-freaking-oke like he's Sinatra.

The dark-haired man with the mic wears a crisp blue suit, a charcoal shirt, and a purple tie I want to tug off.

Whoa.

Bone zone much?

But I'm not really thinking about the bone zone. I'm thinking I want to hear him. I want to experience all of this song, up close and personal.

I weave through the crowd and make my way toward the stage like a groupie. My God, I am a freaking groupie, and I don't care. I push past women in cranberry and purple evening dresses, past men in sharp duds, until I reach the front.

When I'm there, something happens. A cosmic shift, as if the world slows down. As if the room disappears. Everything else is a blur, and I swear there's a spotlight on him, and his spotlight is on me. His dark-blue eyes find me immediately, and when they do, I ignite. This is some kind of dream. I pinch my arm to make sure I'm still real.

Ouch. Yep, I am.

He slides into another verse in the crooner tune made famous by Ella Fitzgerald, Harry Connick Jr., and countless others, singing about music of the night. He pulls the mic closer to his lush, full lips, and—I shudder as awareness strikes me—he sings to me.

Only to me.

Absolutely to me.

I'm not imagining this. He's singing about being young on a night like this to me.

Goose bumps sweep over my skin as the song rises to its crescendo. It's as if I'm glowing, as if he's turned on a golden light inside me that spreads throughout my body with each delicious verse.

When he finishes, claps and cheers resound and fill the ballroom.

No one expected this kind of serenade during karaoke. Who could have expected Old Blue Eyes to get onstage?

The man receives another round of cheers, and a woman in the front shouts, "Encore, encore."

He bows his head humbly and says, "Thanks for listening."

That's all he says. He doesn't bask in the glory or the moment. He walks offstage, and then he's gone. My heart crashes. My shoulders sag. I wanted him to jump off the stage and take me in his arms.

As soon as the thought materializes fully, I'm struck with its utter ridiculousness. I leave a mental note to myself.

Girl, get your act together. He's just a guy singing onstage. Don't think this is going to become some sort of moment. It's ridiculous to even think he was singing to you. He probably picks a woman in the crowd every time he gets behind a mic. That's probably how he makes it through the song.

I take a deep breath, nod, and spin around. That's all it could have been. I was simply swept up and let myself believe it was real. No big deal. It was three minutes in my life and hardly a waste when I enjoyed the hell out of them.

I take the last sip of my champagne and try to clear my head of all these warm, yummy thoughts of a blue-eyed, five-o'clock-shadowed, golden-voiced man with matinee idol looks.

I make my way to the exit, searching for a waiter with a tray so I can deposit my champagne glass. As I hunt, a hand brushes my arm. I startle, turn, and look into midnight-blue eyes that pierce me.

Like in a movie, or a book.

Okay, I'll admit, I'm a certified romantic. I grew up on a steady diet of romantic-comedy flicks, historical romances, and all sorts of delicious poetry. That's what happens when you're raised by a hippy.

But this is fantasy made real. It's happening. His eyes *are* piercing me.

"Thank you for coming," he says, emphasizing *you*. A rush of heat sweeps down my chest. I tell myself to be smart, to be witty, to be clever. But I also need to keep it simple.

"And thank you for singing like that."

His lips curve up in a smile. Oh my, he has great lips. They look soft and full, and I bet they taste delicious. "Did you like it?"

I rein in a smirk, playing with him. "No."

He appears taken aback. "No?"

Emboldened by the night, by the moment, by those piercing freaking eyes, I lean forward and tug on his tie. "No. I was blown away."

Laughing, he runs his hand down my arm. "Blown away is even better than liking it." He nods towards the door. "Do you have to go?"

I tilt my head in a question. "Are you asking me to stay?"

He reaches for the glass in my hand, takes it, and sets it on a tray behind him. It's such a James Bond move. I don't even think I realized there was a waiter next to him. But he did.

"Considering I just caught your

eye in the audience, sang the rest of the song to you, and rushed offstage to find you then catch up with you before you got out the door, yes, I am absolutely asking you to stay."

Backflips. Somersaults. Handsprings. My stomach executes an entire floor routine.

The judges give me a ten for Desire to Stay.

I keep up the coy routine. "True. You did make quite an effort. I suppose, though, if you'd actually run over to me, I'd have said yes."

He snaps his fingers. "Darn. I guess I didn't try hard enough. I guess I'll hang my tears out to dry."

I'm a sparkler inside, lit up and bursting. Like a contestant on *Jeopardy!* I hit the buzzer. "Who is Linda Ronstadt?" I blurt out. "I love her version of that song."

He gazes heavenward, mouths *thank you* as if to his lucky stars, then sets his hand on my back. "You, me, a drink. That sounds like the perfect nightcap."

I don't bother to flirt or play coy this time. "It sounds like a dream."

He leans in closer and brushes a few strands of my blonde hair from my shoulder, making me shiver. Making me heat up.

His eyes find mine once more. "Let's make it come true, then."

3

Sloane

He orders a Scotch.

This seems fitting.

A boy drinks Coors. A man drinks Scotch.

Men who hold their own. Men who sing love songs. Men who don't say *bone town*. God, I hope he's not a bone-towner.

"And what would you like?"

I shrug happily. "I'm a woman of simple taste. A champagne-or-bust kind of gal."

He turns back to the bartender, orders, and then returns to me. "You do look like a champagne woman."

Woman. Not gal. Not girl. I love that he upgraded gal to woman.

"Why is that?"

"A good glass of champagne delights all your senses. It tickles your nose, and it goes to your head, and it makes you just the right kind of buzzed."

The way he says *buzzed*, as if he's telling me it turns him on, sends a thrill through me. A dart of lust. "Is that so?"

"It says you know how to celebrate, and you know how to make every day a celebration."

I laugh. "Wow. Are you a sommelier or a bartender with your drink insight?"

He shakes his head. "I'm just a vet."

I gesture to the setting. "What a surprise to bump into a vet at an event to raise money for animal rescues."

He lifts his brow. "Exactly. Such a small world." He casts a quick look around. "We could probably throw a bone out here and hit ten or twenty vets."

"Do you want to try?"

"Do you have any bones in your pocket?"

I pat the sides of my dress where pockets would be. "Alas, I'm fresh out of Milk-Bones."

"Next time, then."

The bartender hands us our drinks, and he thanks the man then lifts his glass. "To Milk-Bones next time."

I laugh. "Yes, let's drink to Milk-Bone tossing."

He clinks his glass to mine. "Actually, I'd much rather drink to unexpected encounters."

Hope takes flight inside me, as I delight at that toast, those words. "So far, they're the best kind."

A smile spreads, nice and slow on his gorgeous face, and he nods as if to say *well said, well-played*.

I take a drink, enjoying the fizzy taste and the way the drink does indeed go to my head. "So, I'd have thought you were a ringer. Are you really a vet, or were you hired for those pipes?"

He holds up a hand like he's taking an oath. "I swear. I just sing for fun. Besides," he says, gesturing to the stage where a group of five have corralled together to take their turn belting out "Sweet Child O' Mine," "if I were a hired gun, I'd do more than one number. As you can see, I got in line, I took my turn, and now the next group is onstage."

I poke his shoulder. "I don't know if you know this, but you sure can sing."

He offers a smile that says he appreciates the compliment. "It's my party trick."

I run my fingers down his arm.

"That's quite a party trick. And I thought peeling a banana with my toes was good."

He makes a sound like a cartoon character whacked by a frying pan. "Wait." He goes ramrod straight then slams his hand against his forehead. "You can do *that*?"

I'm wearing black open-toed heels, so I lift one and wiggle a toe. "Oh, yes, I can. I learned how to do it on YouTube."

He raises a hand and pretends to call a waiter. "One dozen bananas, stat."

I lean forward, whispering, "Someday I'll show you."

He strokes my arm. "Someday soon."

We can't seem to stop touching each other. We can't stop flirting. The air between us crackles and hums as we chat and drink.

I finish my champagne and decide to go bolder, to tell him what I see in him. I wet my lips, meet his gaze.

"By the way, you look like a Scotch man."

Intrigued, he lifts a brow and sets down his glass. "And what does a Scotch man look like?"

Softly, I run my finger down the silk of his tie. He lets out a slight rumble as I touch the material, and it is the sexiest sound I've ever heard. Like even this small touch from me does him in. "A Scotch man is confident. He's a man's man, but he's a gentleman too. He holds your coat and he holds the door. And he always makes sure a lady is happy."

I hold my breath. Did I go too far? Am I this bold? I'm not entirely sure what I'm going for. I don't think I'm asking him to sleep with me tonight. But I'm also throwing caution to the wind. I'm letting him know I don't simply want to flirt at the bar.

His eyes darken, blazing with flickers of desire. He raises his right arm and curls his hand over my wrist on his tie. The connection is electric.

My skin sizzles where he touches me. He squeezes tighter, like he can feel the charge between us too. "But a gentleman has good manners, and wherever are mine?"

He lets go of my hand and extends his to shake. "I'm Malone Goodman."

"I'm Sloane Elizabeth. Two first names, but one's my last name."

He smiles like that's the best thing I could have said. "You couldn't have any other name. A woman like you has to have two feminine names. Now, Sloane Elizabeth, let me tell you what I'm thinking."

"I'm dying to know." I inch closer to him, the space between us compressing. I'm nothing but electrons and atoms, bouncing and buzzing.

"I'd like to get to know you more. I'd like this night not to end. I thought you were stunning the second I saw you walk across the ballroom. I see that you're clever and even more enchanting the more we connect." He runs his fingers down my throat, touching me so sensually, so tenderly that I nearly wobble. "You seem to have bewitched me."

"I have?"

"And I'm wondering if it would make you happy if we were to get out of here?"

My heart flies high, spreading wings. "Very, very happy."

4

Sloane

We don't hightail it to a room in this hotel. Instead, he hits the button for the elevator, and once we're inside, he reaches for my hand, tugs me close, and says, "Would you like to go for a walk?"

I shiver from his nearness and the sweetness of the request. From the sheer romantic possibility. "A walk sounds delicious."

He dips his face to my neck,

dusting his nose across my skin. "You smell delicious."

My knees weaken. My heart hammers.

His hand bends around my waist, steadying me. "Don't fall, Sloane."

Breathy and a little nervous, I answer, "I'll try not to."

I'm keenly aware of the double meaning. I wonder if he is too.

The doors open at the first floor, and I'm both sad and grateful. While a part of me wanted that moment to unfold into a slow, mind-bending kiss in the elevator, I'm also loving the anticipation, the build. It's a fait accompli that we'll kiss tonight. We both know that, I'm sure. But when it will happen, where it will happen— that's still the great unknown.

I like a little bit of the unknown. I like wondering. I like that he's going to keep me wondering. Because this anticipation between us is intense, seems to have its own pulse, its own heartbeat. I want to keep feeling it unfurl as we go.

We step into the lobby and head out onto the street, turning up Fifth Avenue.

June in Manhattan is its own slice of paradise. The weather is not too warm that you bake, and it's not too chilly that you need a jacket. It's Goldilocks weather, and tonight is just right for a spring breeze and a moonlit stroll.

We head up Fifth Avenue, and as we go, Malone drapes an arm around my shoulders, bringing me in close. I sigh happily as I gaze at the expanse of my favorite city spread out in front of us. "I love Manhattan. I wish I lived here."

"Where do you live? Please don't say Washington, Oklahoma, or Texas."

I laugh, nudging him with my elbow. "What do you have against those states?"

"The same thing I have against Indonesia. They're too far away when it involves a woman I hope lives closer."

Butterflies swoop over my shoulders and down my arms. "You want me closer?"

He looks at me, determination in his eyes. "I want to see you again, Sloane."

"Even though our names rhyme?"

He laughs. "They do. They sound a bit silly together."

"Naturally, we should call this off."

"Fine. The rhyming names are an omen. Clearly, I don't want to see you again."

I stomp my foot playfully. "You really do want to see me again? Already?"

He stops at the corner of the street in front of a florist, tucks a finger under my chin, and raises it. "Yes, and I don't care if our names sound silly together. I do already want to see you again. Is that strange? I like you, Sloane. I already know I like you. I suppose it's possible we could have a

terrible time the rest of the night," he
says, letting go of my chin and
sweeping my hair off my shoulder, a
move that makes my insides pirou-
ette. "But I doubt it. So yeah. I'm a
confident man. I'm confident the next
few hours with you are going to be
excellent. I'm confident at the end of
tonight, I'll be asking you to go out
with me again."

I'm confident he's the sexiest
gentleman I've ever met.

He lets his fingers trail down my
arm to my hand then threads his
fingers with mine, our hands locking.

I smile so wide it can't be
contained. "I have a secret," I confess.

"Bring it on. What is it?"

We resume walking, and I tighten
my fingers around his. "When you ask
me to go out again, I'm going to say
yes."

"Ah, that is a most excellent secret,
and I'm glad I'm privy to it."

As we head up the avenue, passing
pretty   boutiques   and   expensive

restaurants, I answer his question. "Actually, I live in Hoboken. I took the PATH in tonight. The PATH and me are like this." I twist my index and middle fingers together. "And you? Where do you live?"

He points downtown. "A little place in the West Village. I'm hoping to move somewhere bigger if I get the new job that I've been interviewing for. Getting it would be a dream, everything I could want."

"I'll be crossing my fingers that it'll happen."

"Me too. Plus, my cat really wants more room."

"You have a cat?"

He shoots me a curious look. "You say that like it's a surprise."

"No, I just think it's adorable."

"Do you want to see his picture?"

"Of course I do."

He takes out his phone and clicks a few times, and then shows me a big orange cat perched high on a shelf in what I presume is his apartment.

"That's Evil Genius. He's never met a cupboard, closet, or box he can't get into."

"He seems like quite a sneaky fellow. And he's also adorable."

Malone tucks the phone back into his pocket and looks at me. "And you? What do you do?"

"I graduated recently, so I'm part of the vast ranks of young people looking for a job."

"What field are you looking in?" he asks as we reach the Plaza Hotel, where fancy black town cars pull up in front of the famous landmark.

"I'd like to do publicity for a shelter or animal rescue."

He clasps his hand over his sternum. "A woman after my own heart. An animal lover."

I laugh. "I'd think the rest of the people at the fundraiser tonight are animal lovers too."

He laughs. "Don't shatter my illusion, Sloane. I'm pretending it's only us."

I linger on the words—*illusion, us.* Am I letting this magical moment distract me from my mission? After all, I went into the evening only planning to network. I wasn't looking to meet a man to spend an evening with. The last few hours do feel a little like magic though. "Is tonight an illusion?"

We stop on the corner outside Central Park, the moonlight casting a silvery glow across his handsome features. He answers thoughtfully, "It feels a little like one, doesn't it?"

"It does. Like there is a bubble. Or maybe a clock ticking toward midnight."

He scans down the street. "Do you turn into a pumpkin when the clock strikes twelve?"

"Don't be silly. I have a stage-coach. We can take it for a ride."

"Does it go fast? Can we get it over seventy?"

I nudge him. "It goes over a hundred."

"I'm so there."

I waggle a foot, showing him my shoe. "And do you like my glass slippers?"

He eyes me up and down like he's drinking in the sight of me. "Those are the sexiest glass slippers I've ever seen." He steps closer, drops his hand onto my hip, and sinks his fingers to the top of my ass. "And now I'm going to tell you a secret."

"Tell me," I say, breathlessly. I'm thrumming with anticipation, because this is a fairy tale so far.

Of course, that only means one thing—something has to go wrong. Something goes wrong in every fairy tale. You get lost in the woods, attacked by wolves, or left for dead.

Hey, drama queen, settle down.

I will myself to focus on the good, only the good.

To focus on this moment.

A groan seems to rumble up his chest, and his voice goes low and smoky, so damn sexy. "I'd really like to take those glass slippers off you. I'd really like to take everything off you at some point."

At some point.

I like the way he lingers on those words as if it's not something we're going to do this evening, and I'm grateful. No matter how much desire I feel, how much lust swoops through my body, I'm not letting him strip me to nothing tonight. "I think I'd like you to do all that, Malone. At some point."

"At some point, then," he adds for emphasis, like we've found our catchphrase.

We both laugh, and soon our laughter trails off. I glance up at the moonlit sky. "It does feel like an illusion, but maybe it won't end," I say, a little bit hopeful.

He slides his fingers through mine. "The night is young. Let's make it last. You know what I've been thinking about all night?"

My pulse spikes with desire. "What have you been thinking?"

"Where I want our first kiss to be."

He implies there will be more than one. That the first will lead to a second then to a third and then to more. That's the romance of tonight. That's the way to woo a woman. I didn't head into tonight wanting to be wooed, but I want every bit of wooing that he's doing.

I glance up at the moon. "I think right here is a most excellent spot," I suggest.

He surveys the block. "You do? Hell, any place is a good place to kiss you."

I lift my chin and grab his tie, demanding what I want, what I desperately need. "Kiss me, Malone."

He cups my cheek, sweeps his thumb across my lips. I shudder with need.

He drops his mouth to mine and brushes the softest, sweetest kiss I've ever experienced across my lips. I feel it everywhere. I feel it in my hair. I feel it in my fingers. I feel it inside every molecule, the faintest brush of his lips on mine lighting me up.

5

Sloane

He lingers on my lips as if he's delighting in every second of the exploration, every moment of the connection, like a chef would when tasting a new concoction.

He laces his fingers through my hair and tugs me closer, and if I were an old robot in a sci-fi flick, I'd boop, beep, and short-circuit, then fry out.

Because holy overload of sensation. Sweet, hot sparks rush across me, sweeping over every square inch.

My pulse skyrockets, and desire winds its way through every cell.

This man can kiss. And something else I know?

This man wants me.

Badly.

He's pressed against me, the delicious length of him thick and insistent, a tantalizing tease of what's to come.

Namely, me.

In a flash, I can see the night playing out. We go to his place or a hotel. He gets me naked, sends me soaring, and we have pancakes in the morning.

I do love orgasms and pancakes.

But something feels different with this guy.

Not like he can't give me orgasms and pancakes.

But something tells me he's not the guy you go to bone town with on the first night. I bet when I go there with him, it'll be an all-night-long seduction. It'll be moonlight and fireworks and luxurious time spent exploring my body, learning my every desire, pleasuring me until I can't see straight. That's how he kisses. Like a man intent on delivering bliss to the woman he's with. To the woman he wants. And that woman is me.

This feels like it has potential. So much potential to be real. As he deepens the kiss, my mind blurs into the sort of bliss that only an epic first kiss can deliver. It's an unraveling kind. He kisses with his whole body, with passion and fervor and heat.

And I know—I'm certain—he's not a one-and-done guy.

But since I'm a straightforward woman, and I want him to know *my* score, I break the kiss, press my hands to his chest, and sigh happily, albeit a little woozily. "You sure can kiss."

His lips quirk up in a lopsided grin. "It helps that I've been thinking all night about kissing you."

I clear the frog from my throat. "But listen. I need you to know I'm not a one-night stand kind of girl. As much as I'd like to strip you naked and do bad things to you—"

"What kinds of bad things?" He wiggles his brow. "I like bad things. Feel free to elaborate, and please be as specific as you can."

I laugh. "All kinds. All kinds involving lips and mouths and tongues and more. But don't distract me."

He murmurs his appreciation as he wraps his hand around my hip. "You distracted me. You definitely distract me, sweetheart."

Sweetheart.

The term of endearment floods me with warmth, like I'm glowing. I try to center myself and focus on what I'm trying to tell him. "As I was saying, I want to take things slow. If that doesn't work for you, I understand. But it's the only way that will work for me."

He lowers his hands, finds mine, threads his fingers through them, and squeezes. "Let's go to a diner and get something to eat. We can talk as long as you want. And then I'll put you in a cab back to Hoboken. Until tomorrow."

I shoot him an inquisitive look. "Tomorrow? Are you seeing me tomorrow?"

He scoffs as we walk along the cobbled sidewalk next to the park. "Did you already forget? We made plans for a second date, woman. I'm not letting you back out."

I laugh. "I don't want to back out. I want to see you again. I thought that was clear."

He looks at me, a knowing grin spreading across his face. "This whole night is incredibly clear."

I smile at him like I can't hold back. "It's the same for me."

I walk on air to the diner, and I float all through the meal as we chat, and exchange numbers.

After, he kisses me under a street-light outside the restaurant. When he breaks the kiss, he hums a line from the song "I Don't Stand a Ghost of a Chance with You."

I run my thumb across his lips. "But you do."

Then I deliver a soft, sweet kiss.

He presses his forehead to mine, and he whispers, "What am I going to do with you, Sloane Elizabeth?"

Inside, quietly, in the back of my head, I say *fall in love with me*.

Then I wonder where that wild, crazy thought came from. But it came from this unexpected night, from this unexpected evening with a man who sang a most romantic tune.

"I think you should do exactly what you've been doing," I tell him.

He hails a cab, and when it arrives, he opens the door, but then he yanks me in close. "Ah, hell. I need one more for the road."

He hauls me in for a kiss that is neither soft nor sweet. It is hot and desperate and urgent. And I'm sure it's going to piss off the cabby. But

Malone doesn't seem to care as he kisses me ruthlessly, letting me know that as much as he can be sweet, he can be rough. He can consume me; he can be hard and greedy. He kisses me like he's going to leave whisker burn on me, and I want it. I want to be marked by him.

He puts me in the cab for good and hands the cabby enough money to cover the trip and probably a little extra, a tip for the excruciating wait through the kiss. I turn around as the car peels away, and I watch him through the back window until I can't see him anymore.

The entire drive home, I replay the night. I replay every single moment. Reliving *us*. This is the night I want to live in.

I look down at my feet. My shoes are still black. But they do feel like glass slippers.

* * *

The next morning, Piper emerges from her room, yawns heavily, then lifts her brow in curiosity. "Did you network to your heart's content?"

I smile as I brew some coffee. "I did, and I also met someone."

I tell her about Malone, every detail, as we drink our beverages.

She listens thoughtfully, then asks, "And what's next?"

"I'll see him again tonight."

But I can't shake the notion that the other shoe might drop.

6

Malone: Just a couple of quick questions so I can plan for the best date this evening. Are you opposed to wearing knee-high rubber boots for long periods of time?

Sloane: Will we be wading through the Hudson River?

Malone: *shudders* This isn't a horror-movie date, Sloane.

Sloane: Then why on earth would we need rubber boots?

Malone: Oyster shucking, of course, but we'll collect them first. I don't think it'll be too smelly.

Sloane: Did you know that Green Point Fish and Lobster has an oyster-shucking class? Isn't that crazy? There is a class for everything now.

Malone: Would you actually like me to sign us up for that?

Sloane: Oysters are one food I can't stand. Feel free to avoid all oyster-centric dates, now and forevermore.

Malone: Duly noted. Oysters are on the official forbidden list.

Sloane: If you're looking for something new and adventuresome, might I suggest that we try shopping cart races and push each other down steep hills?

Malone: Wow. This is like an X

Games–style date. Should we get on skateboards and ride up crazy-high ramps too?

Sloane: Excellent idea. I'll bring the kneepads.

Malone: I could go in so many different directions with kneepads.

Sloane: You have a dirty mind.

Malone: I absolutely do have a dirty mind, and I'd like to use it with you soon.

Sloane: I'd like you to use it with me soon too.

Malone: Until then, I'll sign us up to go skydiving.

Sloane: Or, wait for it, I have an idea . . .

Malone: Do tell.

Sloane: It's a little crazy, a little edgy . . .

Malone: This is going to be out there. I can feel it.

Sloane: I'm almost too nervous to suggest it. But what about . . .

Malone: The anticipation is killing me. Just say it.

Sloane: Dinner!

Malone: Whoa. How did you just come up with that, like, on the fly? Or, tell me, have you been thinking about that for days?

Sloane: It just came to me. I swear!

Malone: Dinner. Wow. It's almost as if something existed just to provide the perfect opportunity for two people to get to know each other.

Sloane: Is that what you want?

Malone: To get to know you? Yes. Very much so.

Sloane: Same here. I had an amazing time last night. It was almost unreal.

Malone: Yet, I have a hickey on my neck to prove it happened, and I haven't stopped touching it or staring at it.

Sloane: WHAT? I gave you a hickey? When?

Malone: Just kidding. But seriously, I feel the same, and I'd like to speed up time and have it be tonight so I can see you again.

Sloane: I think if anyone ever figures out time travel, it will be the infatuated.

Malone: Is that you?

Sloane: Oh, I'm definitely infatuated.

Malone: I can't wait to kiss you and taste the infatuation on your lips. Until then, would you like Vietnamese, Japanese, sushi, or Italian?

Sloane: Vietnamese. It's my favorite.

Malone: See you at seven.

Sloane: Counting the minutes.

Malone: The seconds.

7

Malone

I wait outside the restaurant, trying once again to make heads or tails of my desire to see this woman. She's been on my mind all day. I thought about her at work, between patients. Hell, she crossed my mind when I went to my second-round job interview at the new practice, the one that looks incredibly promising.

Images of Sloane flitted through my head as I toured the clinic with Doug

Fredericksen, the guy who owns and runs it. I had to shut off the faucet of thoughts when we went out to lunch to discuss the possibilities of working together. He told me he admires my work and could see me on a fast track to becoming a junior partner. It sounds like it could be a perfect job and the ideal next step in my burgeoning career.

Becoming a partner soon would be a dream. Both mine and the one my dad had, which he didn't have a chance to fulfill. The one I want to make come true for him since he's gone. I've talked with a lot of clinics recently, and I've been looking for the right opportunity to take the next step in my career. This chance with Doug could put me on the path to be the kind of vet I want to be, the kind of vet my father was before he died too young.

I want to do all the things he wasn't able to do. That's my tribute to him.

And that's why I'm so damn glad the new job looks like it'll happen.

I check my watch. It's nearly seven, and I'm waiting outside this restaurant in Gramercy Park. I'll see her any second, and the best part is, I won't have to war with my own thoughts. I'll be free to focus on her all night.

She's all that can possibly occupy my mind when she gets out of the cab a few minutes later, looking radiant and sexy in a green dress that clings to her delicious figure, a little black purse swinging from her hand. She wears a grin that says she's been counting down the hours too. For a moment, I wonder how two people can connect this deeply, this quickly?

It happened so fast. So unexpectedly.

I didn't go to last night's event looking to meet someone. I went with some colleagues to show support. And there she was, and I couldn't look away.

Lust at first look? Maybe. But then we talked. Then, it felt like it could be more.

As she strides up to me, her heels clicking on the sidewalk, those thoughts of *what if*, and *what's next*, and *what's wrong* crumble to dust. I reach for her, loop a hand through her hair, and drop my mouth to hers. I claim her lips, capturing her in a hungry, greedy kiss. I can taste that she's been wanting to kiss me too with the same fevered need.

This kiss? It tastes exactly like infatuation. It tastes exactly like I feel, and it goes to my heart.

We break the kiss, and in my best deadpan style, I offer, "Want to eat noodles or spend the whole night kissing in front of the restaurant?"

She tap-dances her fingers up my shirt. "I'm going to need fuel to kiss you all night."

I drop my hand to her delicious ass and squeeze it. "Let's fuel you up, then, woman."

We head inside, grab a table, and order, thanking the waiter. She spreads her napkin across her lap. "How old are you?"

I crack up at the bluntness of her question. "Do I look old?"

She shakes her head. "Not really. Not a day over fifty, I'd say."

I lift my brows. "Wow. The Botox is working, then, since I'm sixty."

She holds up her hands in shock. "Whoa. I want the name of your plastic surgeon."

"You'll have to meet him in a back alley."

"Only takes cash?"

"Only the best do." I clear my throat. "I'm twenty-eight."

She lifts her chin a little proudly as she says, "I'm twenty-two."

"I had a feeling. Since you said you recently graduated. Is twenty-eight an acceptable age for you to date?"

She taps her jaw as if she's thinking deeply on it. "Hmm. I suppose so. Actually, I don't think the age difference is anything. I was just curious."

Then we enjoy the best second date in the history of dates. She tells me she already heard from an executive at one of the rescues, who she met last night, and she's hopeful it'll turn into something good. She's longed to work in animal rescue most of her life—it's her calling, she says.

I tell her that I had a good second meeting too, so we toast to new opportunities.

After dinner, we walk again, strolling through the night, and it already feels like this could be our thing, that we could be one of those pairs of New York City lovers who wander through the city, stopping in front of shops, sneaking kisses, slipping hands into back pockets, touching, brushing.

I don't know how anyone could be so lucky as to meet somebody they share this fast and easy a connection with. But we do. With Sloane it feels like there are no games, there are no charades—we are just two people who like each other and who aren't afraid to say so.

I push those nagging thoughts away, stealing as many kisses as I can, so many they become countless, till we stop in Madison Square Park. We grab a bench and resume kissing like crazy. When it turns into the kind of make-out session where she's straddling me, her back arching, her breath coming fast, I recklessly want it to continue and realistically know it must end.

I slow us down, breaking the kiss.

She looks at me, questions in her eyes, her breath coming rapidly. "Are you sure you're okay taking it slow?"

I stroke her cheek. "Sweetheart, you are worth waiting for."

And the thing is, I know deep down that she is. I'll wait for her as long as I have to.

8

Sloane

On our third date, he takes me to the Brooklyn Botanic Gardens, and we stroll among the flowers, inhaling the scents of tulips and honeysuckle.

As we wander, we do more of what we've done so far. We talk, and we kiss, and we get to know each other. I learn more about his family and how close he is with his twin sister, and he tells me about his friends. I tell him, too, about Piper.

"And what about your parents? Are you close with them?" he asks.

I make a see-sawing gesture. "Mostly. I'm definitely close with my mom since she did the lion's share of raising me. My father and I have a decent relationship. Funny thing— he's a vet," I tell him, then I adopt a serious tone. "Whatever would Freud say?"

He laughs, tugging me close. "Let's hope Freud would have nothing to say on the topic."

"That's one of my life's great ambitions—to be uninteresting to Freud."

"An admirable goal."

We talk about dreams and the things we want to do in life as we meander through the flowers. I'm enjoying everything about this man. Something feels so incredibly right when we're together.

The next evening, we go to a beer-tasting event in Soho, and I confirm my expectations. "Never liked beer. Never will."

"But you gave it the old college try."

When we leave the brewery, I spot a gigantic black-and-white cat lounging on the sidewalk. I survey the block for a person. "Do you think he's lost?"

"He might be," Malone says. We walk over to the cat and the big guy is quite friendly. I reach down and look at his tag. His name is Applejack. "We should call Applejack's owners. He probably shouldn't be outside. Not in Soho at night."

Malone nods as I reach for my phone then dial the number. "Hey. I'm outside the Soho Craft Brewery, and your cat is here." I wait. "Sure, I'll see you in a minute."

Malone bends down, picks up the cat, and holds him.

"They're coming over in a minute to get him," I say.

"Look at you, Sloane. You're a cat superhero."

I point to Malone, soothing the feline. "And you're a cat whisperer. Cats run from most people. This cat runs to you."

"It's my natural animal attraction."

"It seems to work on me too."

A minute later, Applejack's person runs up to us, relieved to have found her cat. "Don't you escape again," the black-haired woman says to the cat, then thanks us profusely. "I swear he should have been named Houdini."

"It's never too late to change his name," Malone calls after her.

As we walk in the other direction, he glances behind us then furrows his brow. "Are you sure you really want to do publicity for a shelter?"

I shoot him a curious look. "Why would you ask me that? It's something I've always wanted to do—work with rescues, getting them as much awareness and support as I can."

Malone hums as if he's thinking.

"I don't think it's a bad idea. But I could see you doing more. I could see you running your own rescue someday. I think it suits you. I think it's exactly a thing you would do."

"Because we called Applejack's owner?"

"Yes, but also because it's what you want. It's your heart. Your passion."

"You think?"

"You'd be amazing at it. Mark my words. Someday you'll do it."

The next night, we go to a piano bar, and we listen to aspiring singers take their turn at the mic. Malone even sings along quietly as we watch. His voice *mesmerizes*, just the same as it did the first night.

I grab his sleeve. "Hey, I think you should be a singer."

He coughs. "I have a job. I'm happy as a vet."

"I don't mean as a new job. As something you do for fun, because you love it. You're constantly singing, always humming under your breath."

He laughs it off. "I have no aspirations to be Michael Bublé."

"But you don't have to make money at it," I say. "You don't have to record albums. Do it because it's something that you enjoy. Do it because it's an adventure."

He arches a brow. "An adventure, you say?"

I nod, excitement wiggling around in me. I can tell this idea is taking flight in him. "You have a real passion and a real gift. Don't let it pass you by. Singing doesn't have to be everything. But maybe it can be just enough to be your adventure."

He drops his forehead against mine. "Being with you is an adventure," he murmurs.

"And I'm glad I followed its path."

We continue our adventures over the next few nights, and during the days, I interview at the rescues. But I keep thinking about Malone's idea.

Start a rescue.

Should I?

Am I too young to do that?

What would I need before I could truly go out on my own?

It's not only the rescue idea that won't stay quiet. I'm constantly thinking of both the man and the possibilities that our life together might hold.

Especially the naked ones.

Because we make a plan—after our seventh date, I'm going to his place.

9

Malone

I walk through the clinic with Doug, who beams and says, "Malone, I feel like we could work well together."

"I do too, sir."

I want to pat myself on the back. I'm glad that he likes my work so far. I can see myself here, building a career and a practice. It's exactly the type of place where I've always wanted to work. It's exactly the type of clinic where my father wanted to work.

As Doug outlines the opportunities and how he sees me moving up over time with an eye to taking on a partnership role, I'm more certain than ever that this job is everything I could want.

When we head into his office, before he even sits down at the desk, he turns around and says, "You know what? I'm not going to keep you in suspense. You're perfect for this job. I'd like to just go ahead and offer it to you."

He extends a hand, and I shake it. "I accept. I'm thrilled."

Thrilled is an understatement. I'm beaming inside.

I sit across from him at his desk as I sign the contract. As we review the final details, my eyes land on a picture frame, and it's like I'm seeing double. As if I've slipped into another dimension. Maybe I have been thinking of her too much. Maybe she's etched into my brain. Because how on earth could her photo be here in his office?

My brain slows. The cogs turn

sluggish. Everything is a blur as I try to process the stunning image of Sloane staring at me. I stare right back at her, unable to tear my eyes away.

"How does that sound to you?"

I blink, having no clue what Doug just said. Somehow, I manage to pull my gaze away from the optical illusion —it must be—on his desk. "I'm sorry. I didn't hear what you said."

He smiles, nods at the photo. "She's quite pretty, isn't she?"

"Yes," I whisper.

"That's my daughter, so don't get any ideas." He says it playfully, adding a wink, like that softens the warning. But the teasing note only underscores the words. He means what he said.

I swallow past a thousand razor blades in my throat. I need to be certain. "That's your daughter?"

Please say no. Say this is a massive misunderstanding. Say you're kidding.

There's no way that Sloane Elizabeth is the daughter of the man who's just offered me the job opportunity of a lifetime.

He sighs happily and picks up the photo. "That's my darling daughter, Sloane. She's a great girl. You'll meet her someday. I'm sure you'll love her."

The trouble is, I'm pretty sure I already do.

My heart is numb. I'm going to have to end the most wonderful relationship I've ever had before it's even truly begun.

That night when I see her, we don't kiss when she gets out of the cab. I tackle it right away. "That job I've been interviewing for? It's with your father."

Her jaw drops. "Are you kidding me?"

"I only wish I were."

She purses her lips. "So what does this mean?" Her voice trembles, thick with tears.

And then I can't resist her. I haul her in for one last kiss. A deep, hungry, needy kiss. A kiss that says *I'm sorry*. A kiss that says *We can't be together*. A kiss that says *I wish everything was different*.

When I break the kiss, I stroke my fingers down her cheek. "Sloane, I've accepted the job. I can't be involved with my boss's daughter."

She nods, taking it on the chin, understanding completely. "That would be a mistake."

"I hope you know I'll always look back on this last week with—"

She holds up her hand, shakes her head. "Don't say it. I have to go."

I let her leave, with her voice breaking, her shoulders sagging.

But what else can I do? Life is full of choices. This is the one I'm making right now. Even though, as she walks away, I already feel like a boat taking on water, sinking in a sea of regret.

Seven years later, I see her on this

very same street where I'm faced with another choice…

Malone and Sloane's story continues in *Satisfaction Guaranteed*, available everywhere!

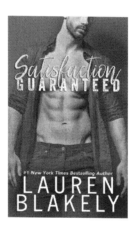

Read on for a preview!

SATISFACTION
GUARANTEED
PREVIEW

PROLOGUE

Dude-bros will tell you the pinnacle of male sexual prowess is to make a woman meow.

I will tell you, that's a dumbass metaphor.

Literal, figurative, it's complete bullshit.

Cats meow when they're hurt, hungry, or just plain chatty. A feline might be stressed, pissed, or simply want you to open the goddamn bedroom door at night.

So, the cat's meow is a myth. I should know.

But the purr? The magical, mysterious, wondrous purr? The aural indication of pussycat pleasure? That's the mission impossible a man ought to be making come to life. Cats purr for a couple reasons, but the most common one is to show they're satisfied.

Yes, *satisfied*.

That's a man's job, and that's why I don't play small stakes kitty-cat games. No cat's meows, no pajamas either. My one goal when I get a woman between the sheets is to make her so immensely pleased that she purrs.

I'm not an over-and-out type of guy. There's no one-and-done for me. I'm a believer in delivering satisfaction in every way, in and out of the bedroom.

That's exactly what I want to do with a certain someone.

Trouble is, that someone is most definitely off-limits, so it's time to put a leash on this dog.

But then I learn something wildly unexpected about her, and there's no way I can turn away from that kind of challenge.

1

She's gorgeous. An absolute stunner, with captivating green eyes, high cheekbones, and strong legs. Her silky black hair is long and luxurious. She stretches, showing off her nubile body.

I can't keep my eyes off her.

Or my hands, for that matter.

I run a palm down her back, and she arches against me.

"Doesn't she seem rather . . . lethargic?" her mistress asks, concern etched in her eyes. I peer closely at the little lady in question.

Those whiskers. That tail. "Sabrina's mood seems fine. Her heart rate is perfect. Her fur looks great. I see one very healthy pussycat. Why do you think she's lethargic, Lydia?" I ask as the silky black feline swishes her tail back and forth, rubbing against my hand on the exam table.

Lydia fiddles with a necklace that dangles between her breasts. "She's not playing with her toys much."

"Does she normally like to play with toys?"

Lydia drags a hand down her chest. "Oh, she enjoys toys so very much."

Dammit. I walked right into that one.

But I'm practiced in the art of deadpan deflection. "Well, that would indicate she doesn't need my services. She seems full of energy here. Is there something else going on at home with her that I should be concerned about?"

Lydia doesn't look at the kitty. She flicks her chestnut hair off her shoulder, her eyes pinned on me, ignoring the vet tech in the room completely.

"She seems to need a little more attention. I feel like that's what she's telling me."

I maintain my completely-unaware-of-her-double-meaning routine. "But *you* give her lots of attention?"

"I do, but it's solo, Doctor Goodman. I think she wants it from others, if you know what I mean."

Yep, I don't need to be Inspector Poirot to crack the mystery of that case. I figured it out the instant Lydia prowled into the exam room with a cat who is as fit as an Olympic athlete.

I slide around her efforts with a standard vet answer: "Cats are fickle. Some want attention. Some are fine without it." Sabrina rubs her head against my hand, cranking up the volume as she marks me. But hey, she's allowed to. Also, cats like me. Dogs like me. I am an absolute animal magnet, and the feeling's quite mutual.

"See? She likes you. She might

want affection from you . . ." Lydia's eyes take a long, lingering stroll up and down my body.

Time for the full-scale oblivion shield. There's a fine line between playing dumb and looking stupid, and as a veterinarian, I can't afford to look bad in front of clients. But as a man, I definitely need to pull off the clueless-to-her-advances act with a particular kind of balance and finesse.

I ask Jonathan, the tech, to hand me a thermometer.

"Of course, Doctor Goodman," he says, hamming it up as if it's his utter delight to deliver the device.

Meeting Lydia's gaze, I brandish the thermometer with a grin. "Sabrina might not be so keen on me after this."

This is the moment when Lydia will back down, I'm sure. They nearly all do when the mercury comes out.

Instead, Lydia emits a sort of *coo*, like a songbird. "Oh, I bet she'd love that. I'm up for . . . I mean, she's up for anything."

Jonathan snickers, and I sigh. I focus solely on the cat, rather than on this cat-and-mouse game of cat-and-woman sublimation. Fortunately, Sabrina's just fine, and I tell Lydia so when I'm through with the exam. I snap off my gloves, wash my hands, and tell her to keep an eye on her feline. "If anything changes, let us know."

She smiles seductively at me. "Oh, I will. My pussycat's health is quite important to me."

Stay stoic, Malone. You can do it. You've done it before. "Yes, I can see that."

She waggles her fingers. "And if anything changes for you, Doctor Goodman, let me know too."

Blank face. I give her the 100 percent tabula rasa. "Thanks for coming in today."

"I'm glad I did." She rakes her gaze

over me. "You're a regular Doctor Doolittle."

I've only been called that, oh, twelve times a day. But it's a compliment of the highest order, so I treat it as such. "Thank you."

She takes a step closer, her stare dropping down, down, down. "Or should I call you Doctor Doolarge?"

I stifle a strangled chuckle—I don't want to give her any encouragement, especially since I do like her cat, as in the actual *feline*. "Let's stick to Doctor Goodman."

After I say goodbye to Lydia, Jonathan clears his throat, adopting a high-pitched feminine voice. "Tell me, Doctor Doolarge, is it *hard* being so good-looking?"

I laugh. "It's the family curse."

"And such a cross to bear. However do you manage?"

"It's not easy. Someday, I'll teach you."

"Yes, please. I want to know all your secrets." He shifts to all-business mode. "You have a few clients who requested phone calls."

I glance at the clock. It's almost closing time, and I have a show tonight. "No problem. I have time."

He hands me the call sheet, and I head to my office and pick up the phone. When I'm done, I swing by the front desk where Jonathan and our office manager, Sam, are debating the best spots for craft beer in the West Village.

"Hey, Doctor Doolarge," Jonathan says, leaning back in his chair, stroking a hand over his bearded jaw. "Got a hot date tonight?"

With her pink hair tied in a huge bun on top of her head, Sam shoots him a skeptical stare. "Don't ask him that. It's personal. You shouldn't pry." She turns to me, adopts a cheeky smile, then whispers, "But tell me. Are you meeting a secret lady at Gin Joint tonight?"

Laughing, I roll my eyes. "Just my sister and the mic."

"But it would make such a yummy story. Vet moonlights as lounge singer and meets the love of his life at underground speakeasy. I can see it now." She spreads her arms wide, making a marquee sign. "They'd want me to play her in the Broadway version of your life story."

Jonathan scoffs. "You can't even sing."

She shoots him a withering glare. "Please don't ruin my daydreams."

I rap my knuckles on the counter. "Speaking of dreams, I have a set tonight then a hot date with some paperwork. In fact, it's the sexiest, steamiest paperwork I've ever seen."

"Just a couple more days, right?" Sam crosses her fingers.

"Here's hoping," I add.

"Me too," Jonathan says.

I head for the door, grabbing the handle.

Jonathan calls out, "Have fun with your paperwork, Dr. Doolarge." Every syllable drips with mockery.

I will never live down this new nickname with my staff.

But if the deal goes through, I can live with it.

What's a nickname when you're about to make your dreams come true?

2

That night at Gin Joint, I sing a Dean Martin tune then slide into conversational mode, tapping a few notes on the piano as I chat with the audience between numbers. "Ever want something so badly you can taste it? Like, on the tip of your tongue?"

A handful of patrons nod, murmuring *yes*.

"And it tastes so good, so tantalizing, it's all you can think about?"

A brunette at a table near the front kicks her high-heeled foot back and forth, mouthing *yes*.

"When I get like that, that's when

I need to lose myself in one particular song." I dive into Louis Armstrong's "What A Wonderful World."

As I play, I'm not only focused on the tune, but on life, and my life is good. In forty-eight hours, my business partner, Doug, will return to town. He's told me he wants to have dinner to discuss a business proposition, and that's why I've been dotting my i's and crossing my t's, prepping the paperwork so I can finalize the deal to buy out his half of the practice.

It's what we've both wanted for the last few years. What we've both been planning for. The practice will belong to me, and I can take it to the next level.

Then I'll have everything I could want: a successful business, a sweet apartment in the Village, and dates whenever I want them.

The icing on the cake is this— singing to a packed house tonight. Fine, that packed house might only be fifty people, but I don't care. I'm not trying to make a career as a lounge singer. I'm just enjoying my second-favorite hobby.

Decked out in a sharp dark-blue suit, I have the audience enrapt with old standards. Men and women sip Moscow mules from copper mugs and gin and tonics from tall glasses garnished with lime wedges. Toes tap in rhythm to the music.

As I dive into the closing number, an update on "The Curse of an Aching Heart," made famous by Frank Sinatra, my eyes land on a trio of women in jeans and black tops, likely on a girls' night out.

A pretty brunette runs her finger along the rim of her glass and bats her lashes at me. Ah, the telltale sign that tonight could be another lucky night.

"You made me what I am today. I hope you're satisfied."

I'm not saying I sing at Gin Joint a couple times a month to score.

I'm saying it doesn't hurt.

Mic and the piano, the perfect

prologue to my first-favorite hobby. But there's something I want more than sex tonight, so I'm going to be an absolute choirboy when my set draws to a close.

"That's the curse of an aching heart," I sing, finishing the tune.

"Thanks so much for coming tonight. Be sure to keep all your loved ones close. I'm A Good Man, and I'll see you again sometime."

I weave my way through the crowd, and the brunette nibbles on the corner of her lips and offers, "I can break that curse."

"Thanks for coming tonight," I say, setting a hand briefly on her shoulder, then make my way to the bar. I'm giving myself a commendation for good behavior.

"Whiskey for you," says my sister, Truly, who owns Gin Joint, as she slides a glass over. "Also, do I need to grab you by the wrists and lead you out of here right away, so you're not tempted?"

"Nah. I'm willingly leaving solo."

She hums doubtfully and lowers her voice. "I saw the gal making eyes at you. Were they full-on fuck-me eyes or were they flirt-with-me-and-give-me-something-to-think-about-later eyes?"

I tap my chin, pretending to think. "I do believe they were take-me-to-your-sister's-office-and-pound-me-against-the-door eyes."

I down some of the drink as Truly smacks my shoulder. "Gross. That's seriously gross. I need to get that image out of my head, stat. Talk about paper clips."

I laugh. "Paper clips are a fantastic invention, not only known for their ability to hold pages upon pages together, but also for their ability to float."

She blinks. "Wait. Paper clips float? Is it because they're light?"

I shake my head. "Nope. It's because of surface tension. The water molecules hold tight enough to support . . ."

She waves a hand. "That's okay. That did the trick." She presses her palms against the counter. "How is everything looking for the Friday night dinner?"

I rap the wood for luck. "If all goes well, the practice should be mine, like Doug and I have talked about for years. At last, right?"

She sighs happily. "We need to celebrate. It's what Dad always wanted for you."

"I know. I'm glad I can finally do it." This has been the big dream since I left vet school—to finish what my father started. To take the step he couldn't take.

"It's going to be great." She pours herself a Diet Coke and raises the glass to toast. We clink and each take a drink. "And when it's all said and done, will you reach out to Sloane again?"

That name sends a jolt through me. "Sloane?"

Truly chuckles. "Yes. *Sloane*," she says, like she needs to remind me. She doesn't—the woman hasn't slipped too far from my mind since that one intense week together that we shared seven years ago. "Sloane, as in the woman you had it bad for once upon a time. The woman you ask me about every time you bump into her, wanting to know if I've discovered some giant loophole that would enable you to pursue her, the woman who's the reason you sing here."

I stumble back, like she just blew me over with the force of her gale-strength words. "When you put it like that, I suppose the name *does* ring a bell."

She laughs. "So, will you reach out to her?"

"Why would I?"

"Won't things change once the deal is done? Can't you finally be Sloane and Malone? Which, by the way, will never not be funny, the rhyming."

"It's a laugh a minute."

"So . . ." Her eyes widen.

I shrug. "Don't know. Hadn't thought about it."

She leans forward, a twinkle in her blue eyes, a challenging set in her jaw. "Liar."

A high-pitched voice cuts in. "Oh my God, are you guys identical twins?"

Truly rolls her eyes. She *is* my twin, and because our coloring is so similar—dark-brown hair, midnight-blue eyes—we've fielded our fair share of this ridiculous question.

I jerk my gaze to the questioner—the brunette.

"It's just that you have the same hair and everything," she says, gesturing wildly from Truly to me.

My sister answers, "Yes, we are. You might have seen us in the *Guinness World Records* as the world's first male-female identical twins."

Her jaw drops. "That is so cool. I can't believe I'm meeting identical boy-girl twins. I thought it was always one gender only."

I point to my sister. "She had a penis in the womb. It fell off before she was born."

Truly tosses a cloth at me while the brunette stares, slack-jawed. "And you became one. One giant dick."

"And on that note, I need to go." I tug Truly in for a quick kiss on the cheek, and then I'm out.

As I head down the cobblestoned block lined with trees, I unknot my tie, humming "The Curse of an Aching Heart."

I'm lost in thought, and then, looking up, I come to a stop.

I have to rub my eyes.

I check my surroundings to make sure I haven't walked into my own dream life. Everything seems abundantly real, from the air I breathe to the ground beneath me.

And yet this is a fantasy bar none.

I've definitely dreamed of those legs,
that body, that gorgeous face.

Here she is, walking toward me.

The one I still wonder about.

The one who got away.

The story continues in Satisfaction Guaranteed

ALSO BY LAUREN BLAKELY

FULL PACKAGE, the #1 New York Times
Bestselling romantic comedy!

BIG ROCK, the hit New York Times
Bestselling standalone romantic comedy!

MISTER O, also a New York Times
Bestselling standalone romantic comedy!

WELL HUNG, a New York Times
Bestselling standalone romantic comedy!

JOY RIDE, a USA Today Bestselling
standalone romantic comedy!

HARD WOOD, a USA Today Bestselling
standalone romantic comedy!

THE SEXY ONE, a New York Times
Bestselling bestselling standalone
romance!

THE HOT ONE, a USA Today Bestselling

bestselling standalone romance!

THE KNOCKED UP PLAN, a multi-week USA Today and Amazon Charts Bestselling bestselling standalone romance!

MOST VALUABLE PLAYBOY, a sexy multi-week USA Today Bestselling sports romance! And its companion sports romance, MOST LIKELY TO SCORE!

THE V CARD, a USA Today Bestselling sinfully sexy romantic comedy!

WANDERLUST, a USA Today Bestselling contemporary romance!

COME AS YOU ARE, a Wall Street Journal and multi-week USA Today Bestselling contemporary romance!

PART-TIME LOVER, a multi-week USA Today Bestselling contemporary romance!

UNBREAK MY HEART, an emotional second chance contemporary romance!

The Heartbreakers! The USA Today and WSJ Bestselling rock star series of standalone!

The New York Times and USA Today

Bestselling Seductive Nights series including

Night After Night, After This Night,

and *One More Night*

And the two standalone

romance novels in the Joy Delivered Duet, *Nights With Him* and Forbidden Nights, both New York Times and USA Today Bestsellers!

Sweet Sinful Nights, Sinful Desire, Sinful Longing and Sinful Love, the complete New York Times Bestselling high-heat romantic suspense series that spins off from Seductive Nights!

Playing With Her Heart, a

USA Today bestseller, and a sexy Seductive Nights spin-off standalone! (Davis and Jill's romance)

21 Stolen Kisses, the USA Today
Bestselling forbidden new adult romance!

Caught Up In Us, a New York Times and
USA Today Bestseller! (Kat and Bryan's
romance!)

Pretending He's Mine, a Barnes & Noble and
iBooks Bestseller! (Reeve & Sutton's
romance)

The Break Up Album, the USA Today
Bestselling standalone
romance! (Matthew and Jane's romance)

My USA Today bestselling
No Regrets series that includes
The Thrill of It
(Meet Harley and Trey)
and its sequel
Every Second With You

My New York Times and USA Today
Bestselling Fighting Fire series that
includes

Burn For Me

(Smith and Jamie's romance!)

Melt for Him

(Megan and Becker's romance!)

and *Consumed by You*

(Travis and Cara's romance!)

The Sapphire Affair series...

The Sapphire Affair

The Sapphire Heist

Out of Bounds

A New York Times Bestselling sexy sports romance

The Only One

A second chance love story!

Stud Finder

A sexy, flirty romance!

CONTACT

I love hearing from readers! You can find me on Twitter at LaurenBlakely3, Instagram at LaurenBlakelyBooks, Facebook at LaurenBlakelyBooks, or online at LaurenBlakely.com. You can also email me at laurenblakelybooks@gmail.com

41489553R00062

Made in the USA
San Bernardino, CA
03 July 2019